Storms

Contents

Written by Catherine Baker

Collins

Have you been out in a storm?
Some storms can be fun.

In a storm, thunder crashes and lightning flashes.

The wind howls in the trees.

Some storms are little, and clear
up soon.
Some storms are big and full of risk!

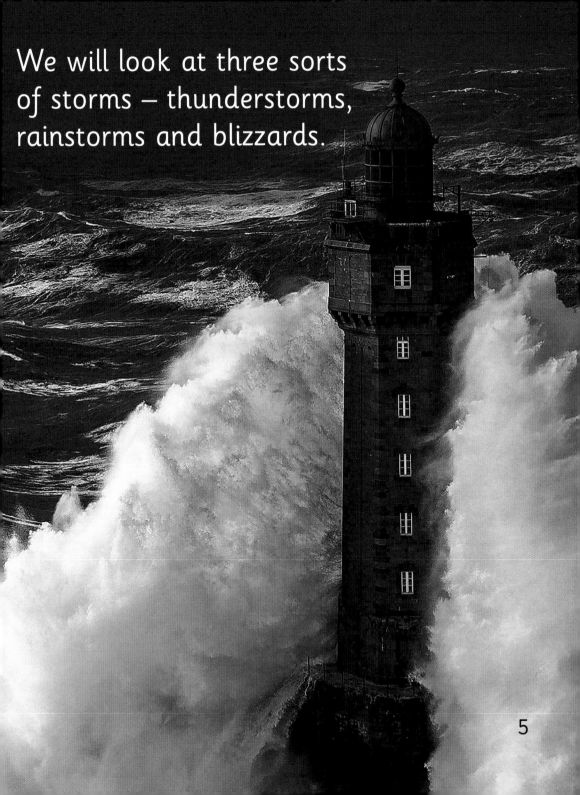

We will look at three sorts of storms – thunderstorms, rainstorms and blizzards.

Thunderstorms

Thunderstorms look fantastic, with bright flashes of lightning. But they can be frightening.

Keep out of thunderstorms!
Lightning zaps at high speeds,
and it can burn things.

Rainstorms

In a big rainstorm, there can be too much rain. Rivers burst the riverbanks.

They can spill into the streets. A lot of things get spoilt!

Blizzards

In winter, blizzards can sweep in.
The wind travels at high speeds.

It is hard to see in a blizzard. It can be difficult to clear a track.

Different storms

hailstorm

Hail is hard. It can hurt!

dust storm

Dust floats in the air.

wind storm

Big trees crash down.

13

Fun or full of risk?

 After reading

Letters and Sounds: Phase 4

Word count: 160

Focus on adjacent consonants with long vowel phonemes, e.g. *trees*

Common exception words: have, you, out, some, the, are, little, full, of, into, be, they, we, there, to

Curriculum links (National Curriculum, Year 1): Geography: Human and physical geography

National Curriculum learning objectives: Reading/word reading: apply phonic knowledge and skills as the route to decode words; read accurately by blending sounds in unfamiliar words containing GPCs that have been taught; Reading/comprehension: understand both the books they can already read accurately and fluently and those they listen to by making inferences on the basis of what is being said and done and vocabulary provided by the teacher

Developing fluency

- Take turns to read a page, ensuring your child pauses for full stops and commas.
- Encourage your child to read with an enthusiastic expression to emphasise the risks or fun in different storms.

Phonic practice

- Focus on three syllable words. Ask your child to sound out the following, breaking them into syllables:

thun-der-storms	diff-er-ent	fan-tas-tic
fright-en-ing	riv-er-banks	

- Challenge your child to find and read two-syllable words in the book.

Extending vocabulary

- Ask your child to think of a word or a phrase that has the opposite meaning to these:

fun (e.g. *boring, dull*)	howls (e.g. *whispers*)
bright (e.g. *dull, dark*)	fantastic (e.g. *ordinary, normal*)
spoilt (e.g. *mended, renewed*)	frightening (e.g. *soothing, calming*)